THE GIRL AND THE BICYCLE

MARK PETT

FOR CLEO

SIMON & SCHUSTER BOOKS FOR YOUNG READERS

An imprint of Simon & Schuster Children's Publishing Division

1230 Avenue of the Americas, New York, New York 10020

SIMON & SCHUSTER BOOKS FOR YOUNG READERS is a trademark of Simon & Schuster, Inc.

For information about special discounts for bulk purchases, please contact Simon & Schuster Special Sales at 1-866-506-1949 or business@simonandschuster.com.

The Simon & Schuster Speakers Bureau can bring authors to your live event. For more information or to book an event,

contact the Simon & Schuster Speakers Bureau at 1-866-248-3049 or visit our website at www.simonspeakers.com.

Book design by Lucy Ruth Cummins

The illustrations for this book are rendered in pencil and watercolor.

Manufactured in China

0214 SCP

2 4 6 8 10 9 7 5 3 1

Library of Congress Cataloging-in-Publication Data

Pett, Mark, author, illustrator.

The girl and the bicycle / Mark Pett.

pages cm

Summary: A wordless picture book in which a girl sees a bicycle she wants to buy,

works hard for a kindly neighbor to earn the money for it, then gets a pleasant surprise.

ISBN 978-1-4424-8319-4

ISBN 978-1-4424-8320-0 (eBook)

[1. Moneymaking projects—Fiction. 2. Friendship—Fiction. 3. Bicycles—Fiction. 4. Stories without words.] I. Title.

PZ7.P4478Gik 2014

[E]—dc23

2013012024